Thomas

GOES TO SCHOOL

by Christopher Awdry

illustrated by Ken Stott

First published in Great Britain 1996
by Reed Books, Children's Publishing
Michelin House, 81 Fulham Road, London SW3 6RB
and Auckland, Melbourne, Singapore and Toronto

Copyright © WH Books Ltd 1996
All publishing rights WH Books Ltd
All television and merchandising rights
licensed by WH Books to
Britt Allcroft (Thomas) Ltd, exclusively, worldwide
3 5 7 9 10 8 6 4 2

ISBN 0 7497 2727 6

Printed in Great Britain by
Cambus Litho, East Kilbride

Every day as Thomas puffed down his branch line, he passed a village school.

As Thomas came round the curve in the line towards the school, he whistled, "Peep, peep! Hello! Here I am."

The children in the playground stopped playing when they heard Thomas and ran to the fence to wave and smile.

"I'd like to go to school," said Thomas to Percy one day in the station yard.

"You're far too big to go to school," laughed the Fat Controller. "And far too useful!"

One afternoon, when Thomas stopped by the school, the children didn't wave or smile. A group of parents and teachers were looking very serious.

Thomas saw there was a large banner hanging outside
the school. His driver read it out aloud: "Save our school
from closing down! Come to our Grand Fête."

On the way home, the driver had an idea. "I know," he said, "I can bring my two donkeys to the fête to give rides to the children."

"And I've got a clown's costume at home," added Thomas's fireman. "I'll come along and make the children laugh."

That night in the engine sheds, Thomas told Percy and
Toby about the school fête.

Thomas wanted to help too. If the school closed down, he would miss seeing the children each day.

The morning of the fête arrived, and the phone rang in the
Fat Controller's office. It was Thomas's driver with some
bad news.

"Both my donkeys have a bad cough," said the driver.
"They can't come to the fête."
"Don't worry," said the Fat Controller. "I'll think of something."

The Fat Controller thought for a while and then went to
the sheds. He told Thomas about the sick donkeys.
"I want you to give the children rides instead."

Before long, Annie and Clarabel were decorated with
balloons and Thomas was given a special polish.
Soon Thomas puffed into the siding next to the school.

The playground was already busy. Thomas's fireman,
dressed as a clown, was making the children laugh.
There were stalls selling cup cakes and lemonade.

There were games to play and competitions to win. But best of all, the children loved the rides on Thomas along the siding.

Thomas chuffed happily up and down the track, pulling
Annie and Clarabel. Thomas was the main attraction of
the fête.

At the end of the day, the Fat Controller counted how
much money they had raised.

"We have raised enough money today to save the school from closing," said the Fat Controller. Everyone cheered.

Thomas was delighted that he had helped save the school.
"Now you've been to school and been Really Useful too!"
laughed the Fat Controller.